CEN
4/21

withdrawn

Blackpool Council

Please return/renew this item
by the last date shown.
Books may also be renewed by
phone or the Internet.
Tel: 01253 478070
www.blackpool.gov.uk

JFP2

First published in 2016
by Jessica Kingsley Publishers
73 Collier Street
London N1 9BE, UK
and
400 Market Street, Suite 400
Philadelphia, PA 19106, USA

www.jkp.com

Library of Congress Cataloging in Publication Data
A CIP catalog record for this book is available from the Library of Congress

British Library Cataloguing in Publication Data
A CIP catalogue record for this book is available from the British Library

ISBN 978 1 84905 683 0
eISBN 978 1 78450 200 3

Printed and bound in Great Britain

From the very beginning...

...everything was scarily

wrong.

Nobody

Seemed to care.

So Boy built a

wall,

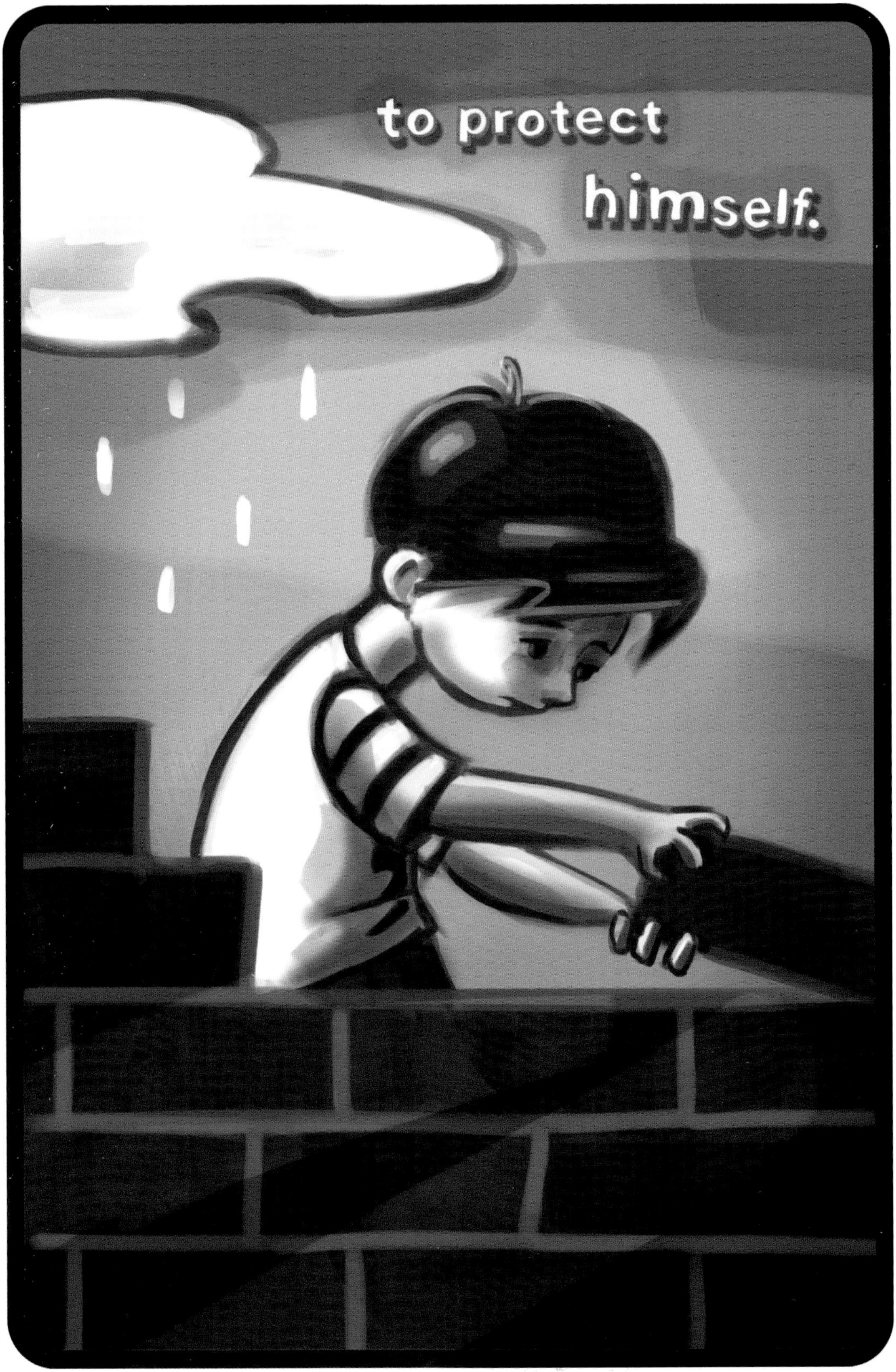
to protect
himself.

But as boy grew,

his wall
became
stronger
and
cleverer.

It helped Boy pretend he was **big** and

strong.

It learned to do things for **Boy:**

Inside, Boy was **sad** and **scared.**

One day, Someone Kind came and asked him where his wall had come from.

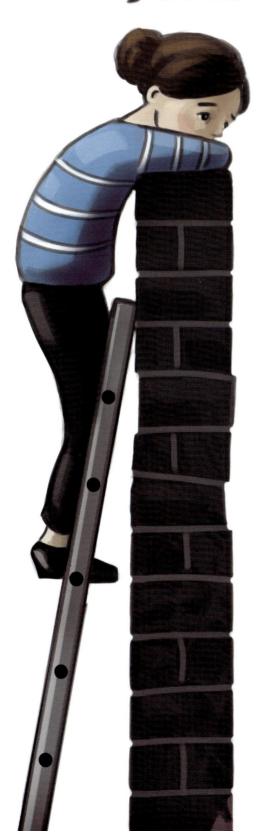

Boy remembered the **dark** time...

...**before** the wall.

He started to **sob** and **tremble** and his wall began to **shake** and **crack.**

Boy didn't like it. He quickly fixed the wall and pretended nothing had happened.
But Someone Kind came back.

She painted the wall with colours

which Boy could hardly see.

Then she made a few holes in the wall and whispered sweet songs through them.

This made Boy angry.

Boy's tears ran down the cracks and into the tiny holes Someone kind had made.

They soon filled and burst into salty fountains,

Each time
he talked
and cried,
a little more of the wall
disappeared.

Soon **Boy** didn't mind the wall **cracking** around him. Bricks were falling about his feet.

Someone Kind
picked them up
and turned them into bridges.

...and

climbed

trees.